Worm Loves Words

by Liza Charlesworth

ISBN: 978-1-338-78271-4
Illustrated by Raffaella Bolaffio

Published by Scholastic Inc., 557 Broadway, New York, NY 10012

10 9 8 7 6 5 4 3 2 1 68 21 22 23 24 25 26 27/0

Printed in Jiaxing, China. First printing, June 2021.

Worm loves **words**!
He can read the book.

Worm loves **words**!
He can read the sign.

Worm loves **words**!
He can read the box.

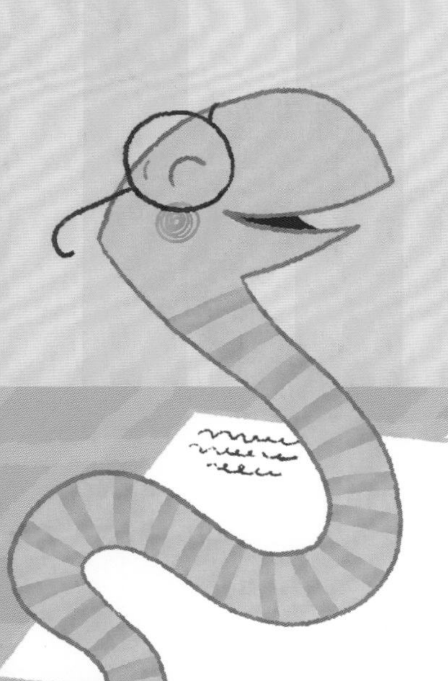

Worm loves **words**!
He can read the letter.

Worm loves **words**!
He can read the mug.

Worm loves **words**!
He can read the pie.

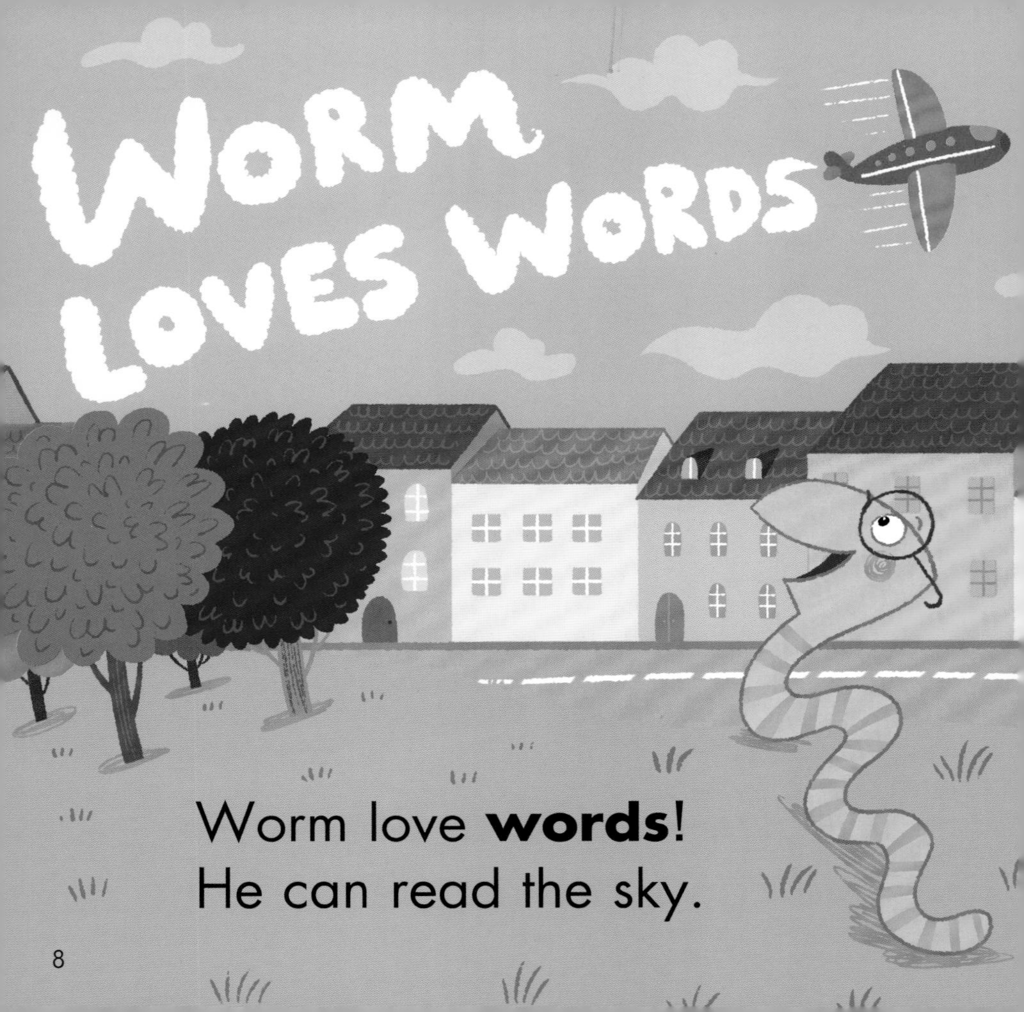

Worm love **words**!
He can read the sky.